To all of the folks at FSG who believe in unicorns, with special shout-outs to Joy, Brittany, Morgan, Monique, and Nicholas

Farrar Straus Giroux Books for Young Readers
An imprint of Macmillan Publishing Group, LLC
175 Fifth Avenue, New York, NY 10010

Color separations by Bright Arts (H.K.) Ltd.
Printed in China by Toppan Leefung Printing Ltd., Dongguan City, Guangdong Province
Designed by Monique Sterling
First edition, 2018
1 3 5 7 9 10 8 6 4 2

mackids.com

Library of Congress Cataloging-in-Publication Data
Names: Young, Amy, author, illustrator.
Title: A unicorn named Sparkle's first Christmas / Amy Young.
Description: First edition. | New York : Farrar Straus Giroux, 2018. |
    Summary: As Christmas approaches, Lucy is excited about the tree, cookies,
    stockings, and especially presents, but despite her urging and example,
    Sparkle is not interested in buying gifts for Lucy.
Identifiers: LCCN 2018001721 | ISBN 9780374308131 (hardcover)
Subjects: | CYAC: Unicorns—Fiction. | Goats—Fiction. | Christmas—Fiction.
    | Gifts—Fiction.
Classification: LCC PZ7.Y845 Uq 2018 | DDC [E]—dc23
LC record available at https://lccn.loc.gov/2018001721

Our books may be purchased in bulk for promotional, educational, or business use. Please contact your local bookseller or the Macmillan Corporate and Premium Sales Department at (800) 221-7945 ext. 5442 or by e-mail at MacmillanSpecialMarkets@macmillan.com.

A Unicorn Named SPARKLE'S
First Christmas

Amy Young

FARRAR STRAUS GIROUX
NEW YORK

Sparkle and Lucy were making a snowman.

"Sparkle, it's almost Christmas!"

They started making a snow unicorn.

"Do you know what Christmas means?" Lucy asked.
Sparkle wiggled his tail and looked at her.

"It means Christmas trees, and Christmas
cookies, and Christmas stockings hanging
by the fire, and Christmas carols.

"But best of all, it means Christmas **PRESENTS!**
Lots and lots of **PRESENTS!**"

"Here's how it works: I will get presents for you, and you will get presents for me.

"Look, I made you a list to make it easier.

"You can use your allowance."

Lucy showed Sparkle where the toy store was.
Then she went to the unicorn store.

She got Sparkle a bottle
of unicorn horn polish.

Meanwhile, Sparkle noticed
some birds near the toy store.

Lucy got Sparkle a box of
rainbow ribbon candy.

Sparkle chased the birds.

Lucy got Sparkle a stuffed unicorn.

The birds chased Sparkle.

Lucy said, "I'm done." She went to get Sparkle.

"Gee, you were fast. Where are your packages?"

Lucy realized that if Sparkle had gotten her a bike or a jungle gym, it would be too big to carry.

"Oh, you probably had them delivered.
That was smart."

When they got home, Lucy wrapped
her presents for Sparkle.

"Did the store deliver the packages yet? If it did,
you can wrap your presents to me. I won't peek."

Sparkle didn't move.

"Or maybe you had them gift wrapped?
Good thinking!"

"Look, Sparkle, our stockings are hung up! And the Christmas tree is decorated! Let's put the presents under it."

Lucy tucked her three presents for Sparkle under a branch.

Sparkle scratched his butt.

"Um, maybe your presents for me aren't here yet? Well, that's okay. You can put them out on Christmas morning."

The next day they went
sledding with their friends
Cole and Shayla. Then they
decorated cookies.

"Tomorrow is
Christmas Eve!"

On the morning of Christmas Eve, Lucy and Sparkle went skating. At night they went caroling.

First they emptied their stockings from Santa.
Then Sparkle opened his presents from Lucy.

Lucy was looking for Sparkle's presents for her, but then her
mom and dad woke up, so it was time to open everything.

"Is that all?"

Lucy looked through the piles of ribbons and
bows and boxes and toys.

"Where are my presents from you, Sparkle?
No presents? That's not fair!"

Sparkle nibbled on the tree.

"Cut that out!"

But Sparkle did not stop. He pulled and pulled,
until he had pulled the whole tree down.

Then he ate the stockings.

GUHUMP!

Sparkle stopped.
He came over and gave Lucy a little lick.

"Go away! You have RUINED Christmas!
You are not my best friend anymore! Do you hear me?"

Sparkle sat down. He hung his head. He sniffled.

A shiny teardrop rolled slowly down his furry nose and splashed on the floor.

Lucy felt terrible.

"I'm sorry, Sparkle."

More tears fell. Big, magical, rainbow unicorn tears.

"You didn't ruin Christmas.

"I can fix the tree. And we can get new stockings next year. Please don't cry, Sparkle. I was mad because you didn't get me anything.

"But you didn't mean to hurt my feelings, did you?
I still love you, and we are still best friends."

Sparkle bleated **"BE-E-E-EH!"** and did a little dance.
Lucy laughed and danced with him.

As Lucy put the tree up again,
she noticed a small package
she hadn't seen before.

"What's this?"

She opened it.

"Oh, Sparkle!" She hugged him tight.

"This is the **BEST** Christmas ever, and you are my **BEST** friend!"

Sparkle gave her a big lick. Then he ate his unicorn horn polish.

"Merry Christmas, Sparkle!"